Oscar's Family

Written by
Melynda Milburn Jamison

Illustrated by
Matthew Walden

For every child who has their own story
of foster care or court involvement and
the wonderful people who give their time
as CASA/GAL volunteers.
– M.M.J.

For my family– the one to which I was born,
and the one drawn around and about me–
each, a loved blessing.
– M.D.W.

Court Appointed Special Advocates (CASA) or
Guardian ad Litem (GAL) programs, as they are known in some states, is a national nonprofit.
CASA or GAL programs use trained and supervised CASA/GAL volunteers to advocate
for the best interests of children in the court system due to abuse, neglect or dependency.
To find out more about CASA/GAL,
and to see if there is a local program in your area, and how you can get involved,
visit **www.nationalcasagal.org.**

ISBN 978-1-66785-092-4

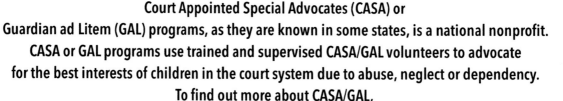

Oscar's Family

Written By
Melynda Milburn Jamison

Illustrated By
Matthew Walden

Today at school we drew pictures of families.

I drew my house, Papa Ben and Mama J, my sisters:

Sarah, Lulu, and Sophie, and Toby.

Toby is my dog.

I also drew a red house and my first mom.

We hung our pictures on the wall. The pictures did not look the same. Mrs. Best, our teacher, said all families look different, but they are all beautiful.
I liked looking at all the pictures.
Katie's picture even had a pig!

After school, I took my picture home and showed Mama J. I told her all about it, and told her that the red house was my first mom's house.

I told Mama J sometimes I feel sad, because I can't see my first mom.

Mama J hugged me and said it was okay to feel sad.
She said she feels sad sometimes too. Mama J is my
foster mom and Papa Ben is my foster dad. My sisters
and I went to live with them, because my first mom
can't take care of us or keep us safe right now.
I guess that makes Toby my foster dog.

Mama J said
family doesn't have to live
together or even look alike.
She said family is people who
love each other and
take care of each other.
I told her that meant
I needed a bigger piece
of paper, so I could
draw the rest
of my family.

I drew Nana, Papaw, Grandma, Uncle Mike, and my cousins. I'm lucky to have so many people who love me and help take care of me. I also drew Ms. Liz.

Ms. Liz is my CASA.
She visits me and my sisters and talks to us.
She is very nice and likes to play games and read books with us. She also talks to Mama J, Papa Ben, and sometimes my teacher.

Mama J says the judge is the person who decides where I live. Ms. Liz says she tells the judge how my sisters and I are doing. The judge likes to hear about school, how much I am growing, and if I'm happy.

Ms. Liz said the judge really liked to hear about my race car birthday party last month.

Sometimes when Ms. Liz comes to visit us, she brings Matilda. Matilda is a special dog that can do lots of tricks. Ms. Liz calls the tricks "commands". Matilda is a lot bigger than Toby and doesn't bark like other dogs.

Matilda went to a special school for dogs.
(I wonder if it was like my school.)
She can shake, lay on my lap,
close the door, and even
bring me a tissue
when I am sad.
I like when Matilda
comes to see me,
because she is
so soft, and
she walks
beside me.

I used the yellow crayon to add Matilda to my drawing.
She is definitely part of my family. My picture makes me proud.
I have so many people and animals who love me and help take
care of me. Mama J hung my picture on the refrigerator.
She said she was proud of me, too.

When I went to sleep, I dreamed about all the special people in my family. In my dream we went swimming at the pool, went to the park, read books, and played with my sisters.

When I woke up, Mama J told me
it was my turn to take something to school
for Show and Tell. I thought about taking my
blue monster truck or my favorite ball
to play catch with.

Then I saw my drawing on the refrigerator.

I told Mama J that
I wanted to take my new
drawing to show all my friends.
She said it was a great idea and
quickly made a phone call.

I rolled up my drawing and took it to school in my backpack. After lunch, my teacher said it was time for Show and Tell and today was my turn! Everyone went to the carpet and sat down.

There was a knock on the classroom door and Mrs. Best said someone was here to see me. I ran to the door and it was Ms. Liz and Matilda!

Ms. Liz said Mama J called her about Show and Tell and she and Matilda wanted to come.

I ran back to the carpet with Matilda.
I told her to sit and she did.
I climbed into the big green
Show and Tell chair.

I unrolled my drawing
and told my friends,
    "This picture is my family.
    It has Mama J, Papa Ben,
        Sarah, Lulu, Sophie, Toby,
            Ms. Liz, Matilda,
                my first mom,
                Nana, Papaw, Grandma,
    Uncle Mike, and my cousins."
I told my friends that family doesn't have to look alike
or even live together. I said I needed a bigger paper because I have
so many people who love me and help take care of me.

Then I told them how Matilda is a special dog. Ms. Liz helped me show my friends how Matilda can do commands. I told my friends Matilda is part of my family because she always loves me, when I'm happy or even when I'm grumpy.

Cameron and Bella
asked questions about
my family and especially
about Matilda.
Then everyone clapped
and thanked me
for sharing about my family.
As I rolled up my drawing,
I felt like the luckiest boy in the world!

Melynda Milburn Jamison

lives in Kentucky and considers herself blessed
to continually need a larger piece of paper to contain
those who comprise her family. Many of those special
people are included in this book. This is her first book and
she hopes it inspires more people to become
CASA/GAL volunteers.

Matthew Walden

loves the hills and mountains of his
native Tennessee home and those of Washington State,
and the family in all points in between. He enjoys drawing,
and hopes that his pictures will inspire others to join in the
act of creation and bringing good things into the world.